Daddies

By JANET FRANK

Illustrated by
TIBOR GERGELY

A GOLDEN BOOK • NEW YORK

This 2011 edition published in the United States by Golden Books, an imprint of Random House Children's Books, a division of Random House, Inc., 1745 Broadway, New York, NY 10019. Originally published in slightly different form in the United States by Simon and Schuster, Inc., and Artists and Writers Guild, Inc., in 1953. Golden Books, A Golden Book, A Little Golden Book, the G colophon, and the distinctive gold spine are registered trademarks of Random House, Inc. A Little Golden Book Classic is a trademark of Random House, Inc.

www.randomhouse.com/kids

Educators and librarians, for a variety of teaching tools, visit us at www.randomhouse.com/teachers

Library of Congress Control Number: 2009937300

ISBN: 978-0-375-86130-7

Printed in the United States of America

20 19 18 17 16 15 14 13 12 11

What do Daddies do all day?
Daddies work while children play.

They work at desks.

They work in stores,

in factories

and out-of-doors.

Some Daddies help us keep well-fed.
They make buns and cakes and bread.

Some build planes.

Some make them fly.

Some catch fish for us to fry.

Dads make clocks

and Dads make chairs.

Farmer Dads grow corn and pears.

Dads are sailors dressed in blue.

And Daddies are policemen, too.

Dads dig coal

and Dads drive cars.

Dads put food in cans and jars.

Doctor Daddies keep folks well.

Daddies paint

and Daddies sell.

Daddies sit at desks and write

the books we read in bed each night.

Dads make steel

and Daddies sing.

Dads do almost everything.

But when they've worked the whole day through, what do they like best to do?

By taxi, train, by car and bus,

Daddy rushes home—

to us!